Dear Parent:
Your child's love of reading s   here!

Every child learns to read in a different way and at his or her own speed. Some go back and forth between reading levels and read favorite books again and again. Others read through each level in order. You can help your young reader improve and become more confident by encouraging his or her own interests and abilities. From books your child reads with you to the first books he or she reads alone, there are I Can Read Books for every stage of reading:

SHARED READING
Basic language, word repetition, and whimsical illustrations, ideal for sharing with your emergent reader

BEGINNING READING
Short sentences, familiar words, and simple concepts for children eager to read on their own

READING WITH HELP
Engaging stories, longer sentences, and language play for developing readers

READING ALONE
Complex plots, challenging vocabulary, and high-interest topics for the independent reader

ADVANCED READING
Short paragraphs, chapters, and exciting themes for the perfect bridge to chapter books

I Can Read Books have introduced children to the joy of reading since 1957. Featuring award-winning authors and illustrators and a fabulous cast of beloved characters, I Can Read Books set the standard for beginning readers.

A lifetime of discovery begins with the magical words **"I Can Read!"**

Visit www.icanread.com for information
on enriching your child's reading experience.

Spider-Man versus Hydro-Man
© 2011 Marvel Entertainment LLC and its subsidiaries. MARVEL, Spider-Sense, Spider-Man: ™ and © 2011 Marvel Entertainment, LLC, and its subsidiaries. Licensed by Marvel Characters B.V. www.marvel.com. All rights reserved. Printed in the United States of America. No part of this book may be used or reproduced in any manner whatsoever without written permission except in the case of brief quotations embodied in critical articles and reviews. For information address HarperCollins Children's Books, a division of HarperCollins Publishers, 10 East 53rd Street, New York, NY 10022.
www.icanread.com

Library of Congress catalog card number: 2010936390
ISBN 978-0-06-162629-6
Typography by Joe Merkel

12   13   LP/WOR   10 9 8 7 6 5   ❖   First Edition

SPIDER SENSE
SPIDER-MAN

Spider-Man
versus Hydro-Man

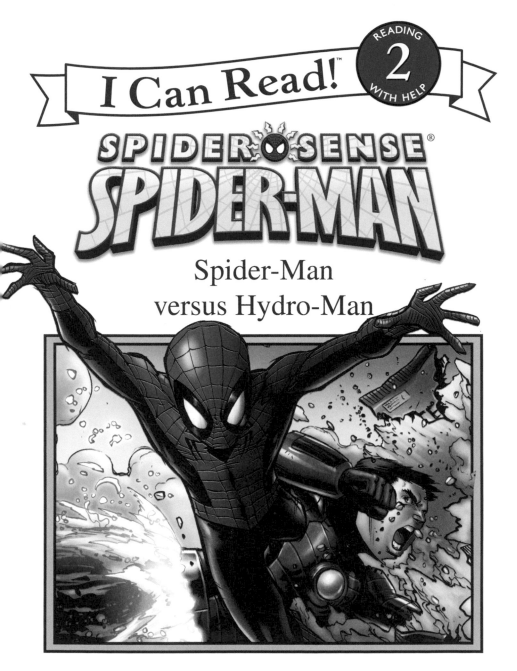

by Susan Hill
pictures by Andie Tong
colors by Jeremy Roberts

HARPER
An Imprint of HarperCollinsPublishers

HYDRO-MAN

Hydro-Man can change any part of his body into water. He is one of Spider-Man's worst enemies.

SPIDER-MAN

Peter Parker has a secret identity. He is Spider-Man!

It was another hot day,
and Spider-Man was on patrol.
Something strange was going on.
Almost all the drinking water
in Manhattan was gone.
The city was at a standstill.

Suddenly the hero's spider-sense

began to tingle.

"Hydro-Man!" said Spider-Man.
"Of course that Wet Threat
is behind this dry spell!"

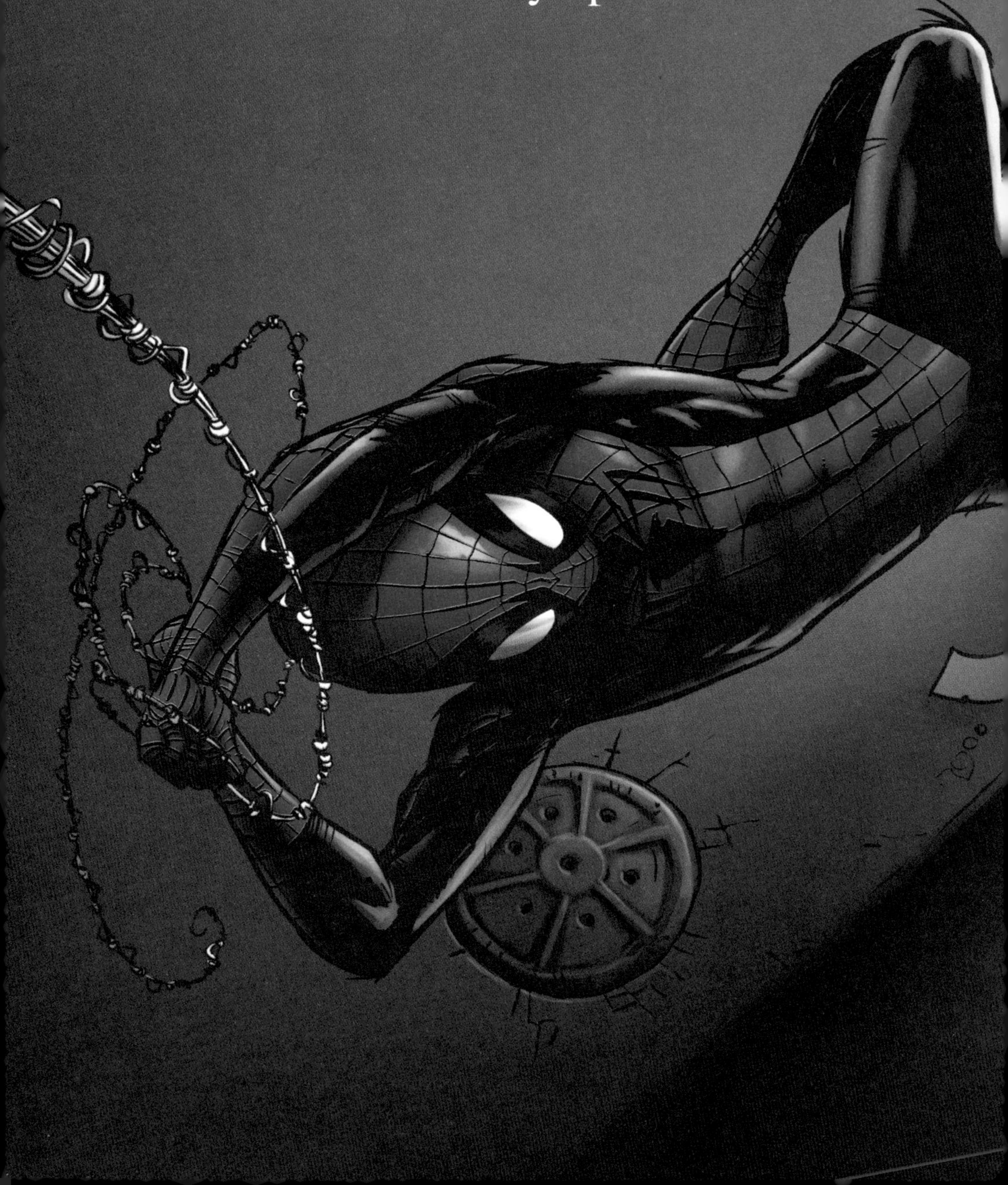

"That's right, Itsy-Bitsy,"
Hydro-Man hissed.
"I'm going to
wash this spider out!"

"Oh, dry up, Hydro," said Spidey,

"Let the city have its water back."

"Give it back?

Why? So everyone can waste it again?

Never!

Soon I'll have every last drop."

"Nice plan, Hydro,
but I think it's sprung a leak,"
said Spidey.

"You are too late, Spider-Man,"
Hydro roared.

"I am not going to let anything
stop me now!"

Spidey was caught by a blast of water
and knocked off his feet.

Spider-Man could hear Hydro laughing

as he escaped.

"I've got to follow him," Spidey said.

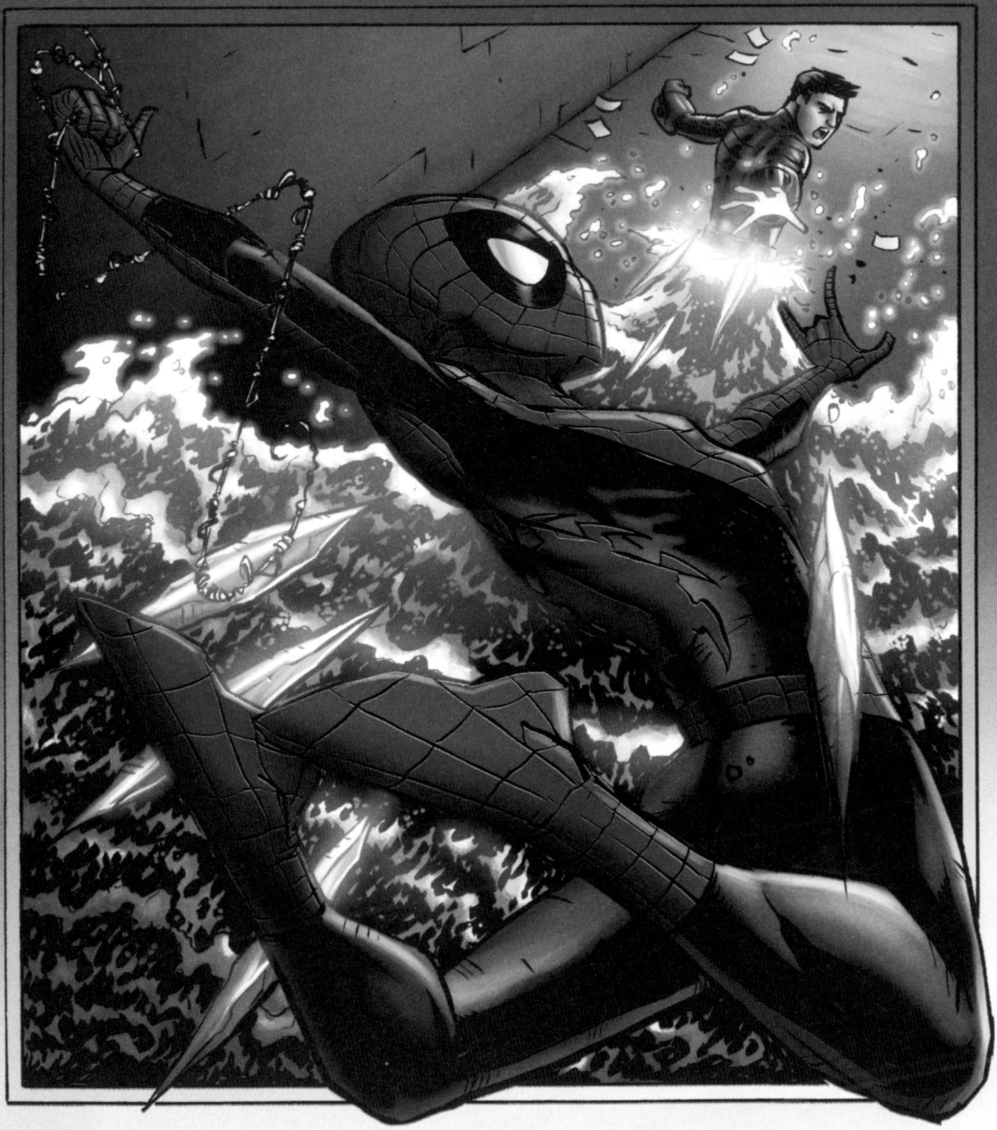

The hero followed Hydro-Man,
shooting webs and
dodging more water attacks.

Hydro-Man was fed up
with this pesky bug.
He swirled around angrily
and fired a huge water bomb.

Hydro-Man escaped down a storm grate and went into the sewers.

Spider-Man had no choice
but to follow him.
"Yuck," said Spidey as he landed
in the dirty water.

Hydro-Man soaked up the sewer water
and turned into a huge wave.

"I'll flush you down the drain,"
Hydro-Man yelled!
The filthy sewer water
rushed toward Spider-Man.

Spidey tried to escape
but the wall of water was too quick

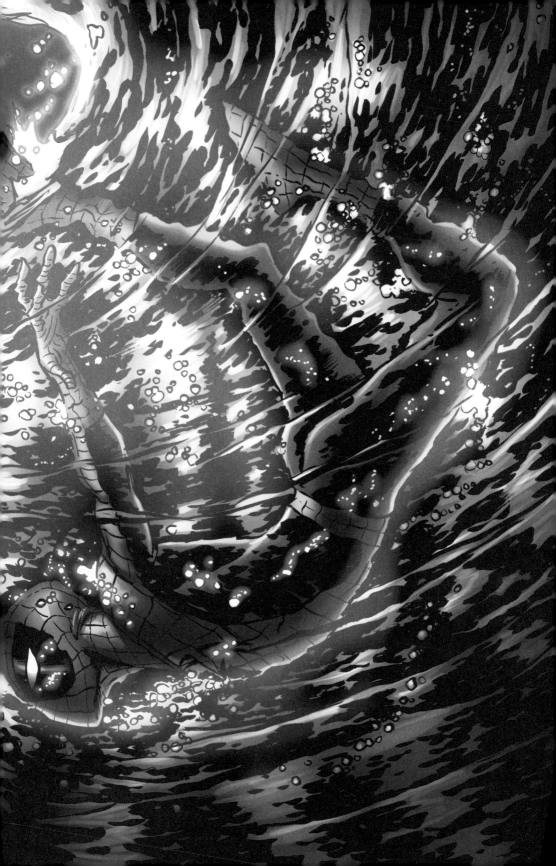

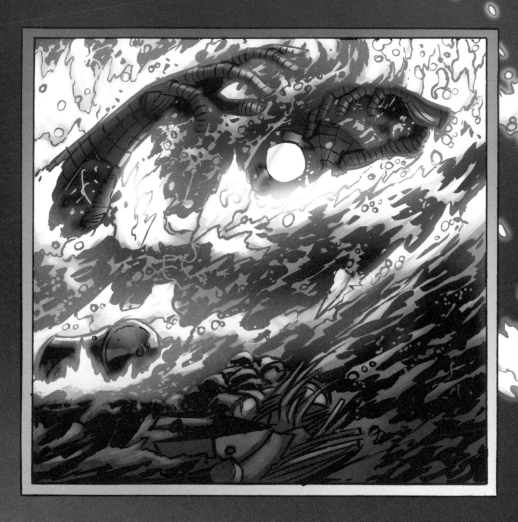

Spidey gasped for air as he was rushed
along in the torrent.

He needed to think of a way out of
this mess!

Suddenly the sewer tunnel turned sharply.

There was only one way
for all that rushing water to go.

Spider-Man blasted out of a manhole.

"Now I'll mop the floor with you, Spider-Man!" Hydro roared.

"Not to rain on your parade,
but you have to catch me first,"
Spider-Man said.

Spidey swung as fast as he could.

He led Hydro to a building site.

"Now I've got you, Spider-Man,"

Hydro roared.

"You're about to be all washed up."

But Spidey had other plans.

CEMENT

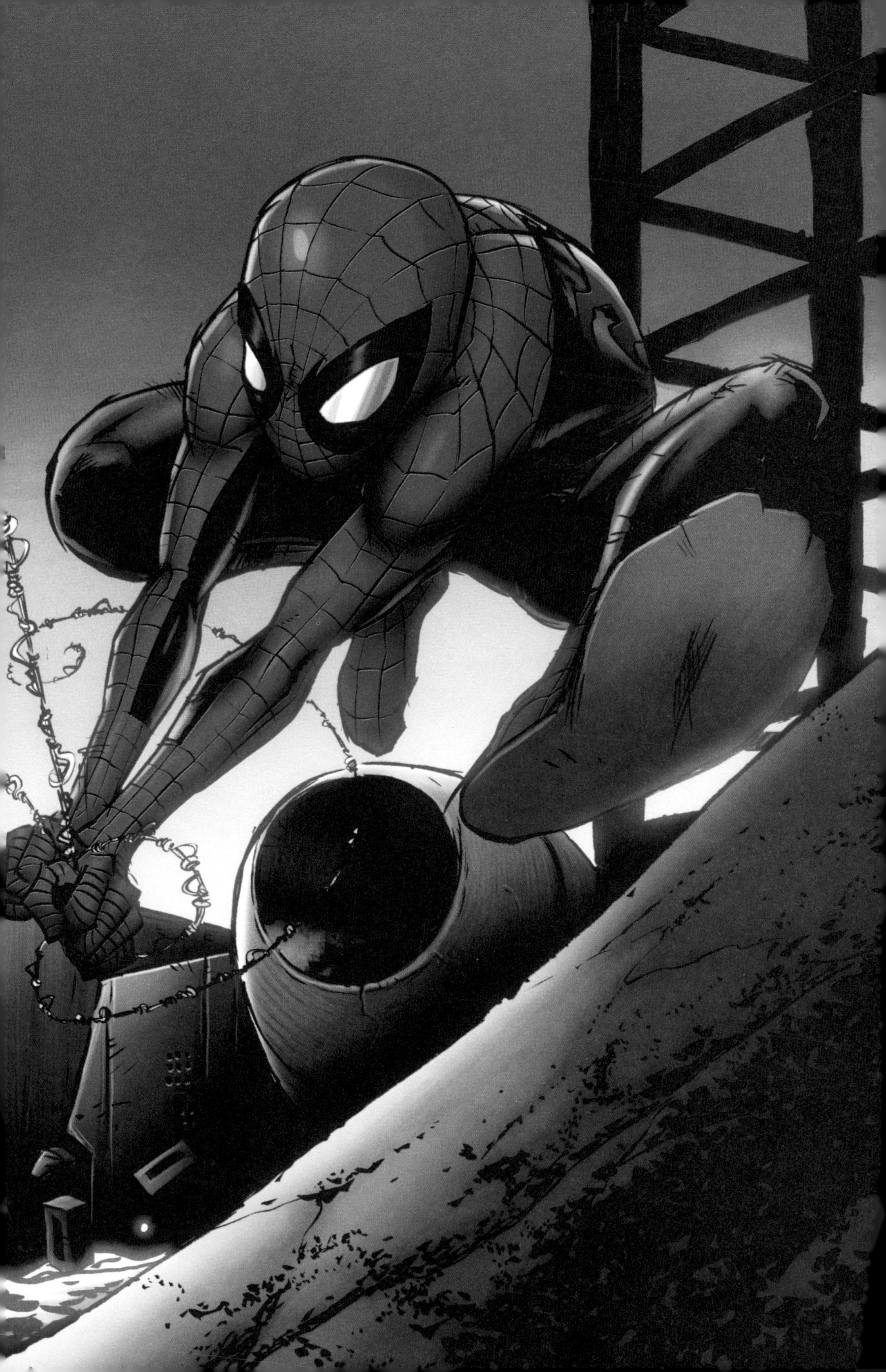

Hydro-Man blasted himself
at Spider-Man.

At the last second,
Spidey swung out of the way.

Behind him was dry cement.

Hydro-Man mixed with the cement
and dried instantly in the hot sun.

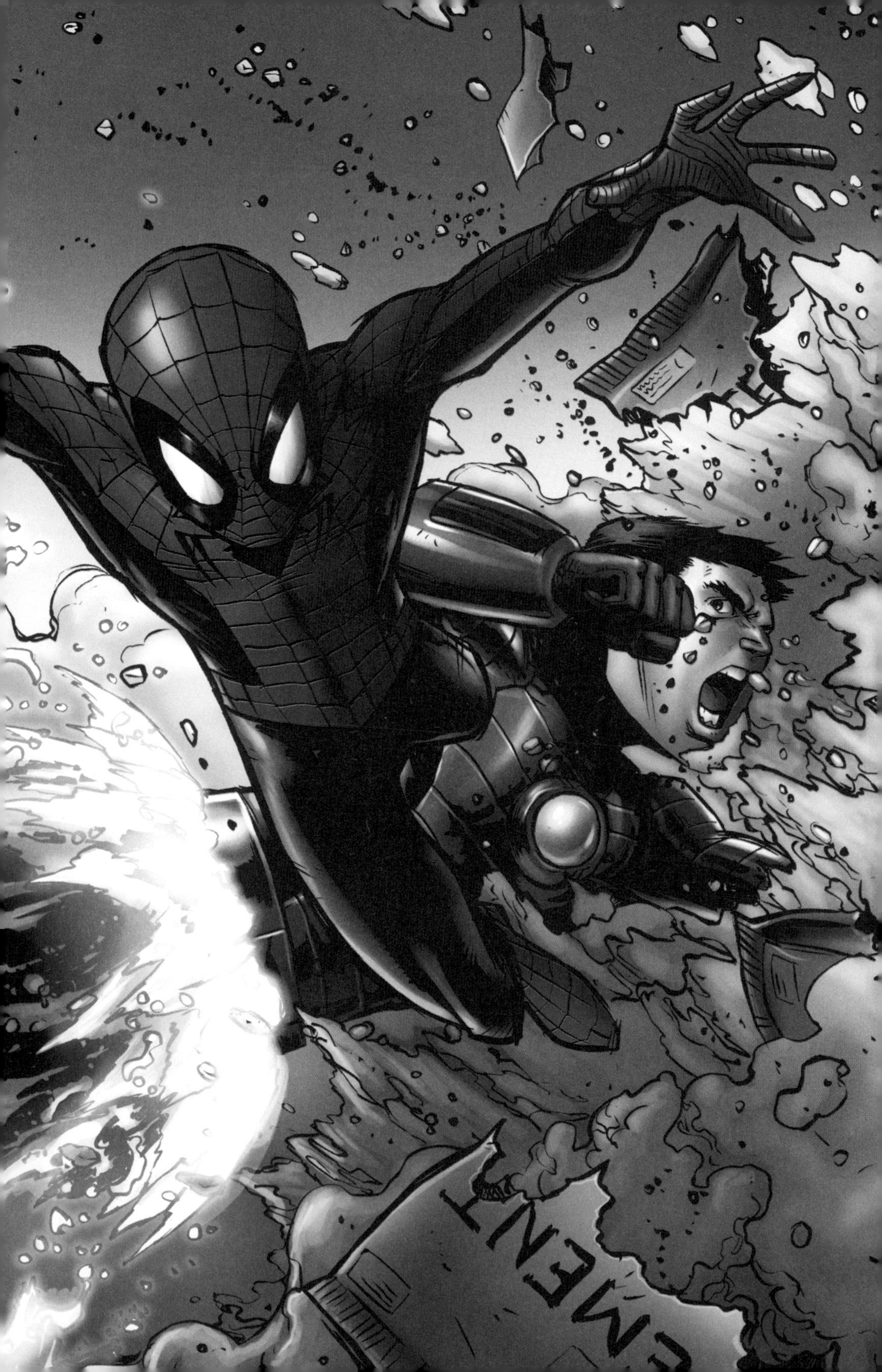

The police took Hydro-Man away.

The city could finally have its water back.

Spidey was the hero—again.

"Now that was one hard case,"

Spidey said as he swung away.